HORRiD HENRY
and the
Demon Dinner Lady

HORRiD HENRY
and the
Demon Dinner
Lady

Francesca Simon
Illustrated by Tony Ross

Orion
Children's Books

Horrid Henry and the Demon Dinner Lady originally appeared in
Horrid Henry's Revenge first published in
Great Britain in 2001 by Orion Children's Books
This edition first published in Great Britain in 2013
by Orion Children's Books
a division of the Orion Publishing Group Ltd
Orion House
5 Upper Saint Martin's Lane
London WC2H 9EA
An Hachette UK Company

1 3 5 7 9 10 8 6 4 2

ISBN 978 1 4440 0120 4
Printed in China

www.orionbooks.co.uk
www.horridhenry.co.uk

For Clare
Spottiswoode and
Oliver Richards

There are many more **Horrid Henry** books available.
For a complete list visit
www.horridhenry.co.uk
or
www.orionbooks.co.uk

Contents

Chapter 1

"You're not having a packed lunch
and that's final," yelled Dad.

"It's not fair!" yelled Horrid Henry.
"Everyone in my class has a
packed lunch."

"N-O spells no," said Dad.
"It's too much work. And you never
eat what I pack for you."

"But I hate school dinners!"
screamed Henry.
"I'm being poisoned!"
He clutched his throat.

"Dessert today was – blecccch –
fruit salad! And it had worms
in it! I can feel them slithering
in my stomach – uggghh!"

Horrid Henry fell to the floor,
gasping and rasping.

Mum continued watching TV.
Dad continued watching TV.

"I love school dinners,"
said Perfect Peter.
"They're so nutritious and delicious.
Especially those lovely spinach salads."

"Shut up, Peter!"
snarled Henry.

"Muuuum!"
wailed Peter.
"Henry told me
to shut up!"

"Don't be horrid, Henry!"
said Mum. "You're not having a
packed lunch and that's that."

Chapter 2

Horrid Henry and his parents had been fighting about packed lunches for weeks. Henry was desperate to have a packed lunch.

Actually, he was desperate
not to have a school dinner.
Horrid Henry hated school dinners.
The stinky smell.

The terrible way Sloppy Sally
ladled food *splat!* on his tray so that
most of it splashed all over him.

And the food! Queuing for hours
for revolting ravioli and squashed
tomatoes. The lumpy custard.
The blobby mashed potatoes.
Horrid Henry could not bear it
any longer.

"Oh please," said Henry.
"I'll make the packed lunch myself."
Wouldn't that be great! He'd fill his
lunchbox with four packs of crisps,
chocolate, doughnuts, cake, lollies,
and one grape.

Now that's what
I call a real lunch, thought Henry.

Mum sighed.
Dad sighed.
They looked at each other.

"If you promise that everything
in your lunchbox will get eaten,
then I'll do a packed lunch for you,"
said Dad.

"Oh thank you thank you thank
you!" said Horrid Henry.
"Everything will get eaten,
I promise."

Just not by me, he thought gleefully.
Packed lunch room, here I come.
Food fights, food swaps,
food fun at last.

Yippee!

Chapter 3

Horrid Henry strolled into the packed lunch room.

He was King Henry the Horrible,
surveying his unruly subjects.
All around him children were
screaming and shouting, pushing
and shoving, throwing food
and trading treats.
Heaven!

Horrid Henry smiled happily
and opened his Terminator Gladiator
lunchbox.
Hmmm. An egg salad sandwich.
On brown bread. With crusts. Yuck!
But he could always swap it for one
of Greedy Graham's stack
of chocolate spread sandwiches.
Or one of Rude Ralph's jam rolls.

That was the great thing about
packed lunches, thought Henry.
Someone always wanted what
you had. No one ever wanted
someone else's school dinner.
Henry shuddered.

But those bad days were behind him,
part of the dim and distant past.
A horror story to tell his
grandchildren.

Henry could see it now. A row of
horrified toddlers, screaming and
crying while he told terrifying tales
of stringy stew and soggy semolina.

Now, what else?
Henry's fingers closed on something
round. An apple. Great, thought
Henry, he could use it for target
practice, and the carrots would
be perfect for poking Gorgeous
Gurinder when she wasn't looking.

Henry dug deeper.
What was buried right at the
bottom? What was hidden under the
celery sticks and the granola bar?
Oh boy! Crisps!

Henry loved crisps.

So salty!

So crunchy!

So yummy!

His mean, horrible parents only
let him have crisps once a week.
Crisps! What bliss! He could taste
their delicious saltiness already.

He wouldn't share them with anyone,
no matter how hard they begged.
Henry tore open the bag
and reached in . . .
Suddenly a huge shadow fell over
him. A fat greasy hand shot out.
Snatch! Crunch. Crunch.
Horrid Henry's crisps were gone.

Henry was so shocked that for a
moment he could not speak.
"Wha – wha – what was that?"
gasped Henry as a gigantic woman
waddled between the tables.
"She just stole my crisps!"

"That,"
said Rude Ralph
grimly, "was Greta.
She's the demon
dinner lady."

"Watch out
for her!"
squealed
Sour Susan.

"She's the
sneakiest snatcher
in school," wailed
Weepy William.

What?
A dinner lady who snatched food
instead of dumping it on your plate?
How could this be?

Chapter 4

Henry stared as Greasy Greta
patrolled up and down the aisles.
Her piggy eyes darted from
side to side.

She ignored Aerobic Al's carrots.

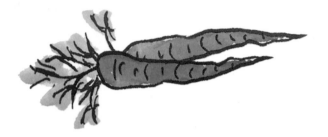

She ignored Tidy
Ted's yoghurt.

She ignored
Goody–Goody
Gordon's orange.

Then suddenly . . .

Snatch! Chomp. Chomp.

Sour Susan's sweets were gone.

Snatch! Chomp. Chomp.
Dizzy Dave's doughnut was gone.

Snatch! Chomp. Chomp.
Beefy Bert's biscuits were gone.

Moody Margaret looked up
from her lunch.

"Don't look up!" shrieked Susan.

Too late! Greasy Greta swept
Margaret's food away, stuffing
Margaret's uneaten chocolate bar
into her fat wobbly cheeks.

"Hey, I wasn't finished!"
screamed Margaret. Greasy Greta
ignored her and marched on.

Weepy William tried to hide his
toffees under his cheese sandwich.
But Greasy Greta wasn't fooled.

Snatch! Gobble. Gobble.

The toffees vanished down
Greta's gaping gob.

"Waaah," wailed William.
"I want my toffees!"

"No sweets in school,"
barked Greasy Greta.

She marched up and down,
up and down, snatching and grabbing,
looting and devouring, wobbling
and gobbling.

Why had no one told him there was a demon dinner lady in charge of the packed lunch room?

Chapter 5

"Why didn't you warn me about her, Ralph?" demanded Henry.

Rude Ralph shrugged.
"It wouldn't have done any good.
She is unstoppable."
We'll see about that, thought Henry.
He glared at Greta. No way would
Greasy Greta grab his food again.

On Tuesday Greta snatched
Henry's doughnut.

On Wednesday Greta snatched
Henry's cake.

On Thursday Greta snatched
Henry's biscuits.

On Friday, as usual, Horrid Henry
persuaded Anxious Andrew to swap
his crisps for Henry's granola bar.
He persuaded Kung-Fu Kate to swap
her chocolates for Henry's raisins.
He persuaded Beefy Bert to swap his
biscuits for Henry's carrots.

But what was the use of being such a
brilliant food trader, thought Henry
miserably, if Greasy Greta
just swooped and snaffled his
hard-won treats?

Henry tried hiding
his desserts.

He tried eating his
desserts secretly.

He tried tugging
them back.

But it was no use.

The moment he snapped open
his lunch box – SNATCH!
Greasy Greta grabbed the goodies.
Something had to be done.

Chapter 6

"Mum," complained Henry, "there's a demon dinner lady at school snatching our sweets."

"That's nice, Henry," said Mum, reading her newspaper.

"Dad," complained Henry,
"there's a demon dinner lady at
school snatching our sweets."

"Good," said Dad.
"You eat too many sweets."

"We're not allowed to bring sweets to school, Henry," said Perfect Peter.

"But it's not fair!" squealed Henry. "She takes crisps, too."

"If you don't like it, go back to school dinners," said Dad.

"No!" howled Henry.
"I hate school dinners!"

Watery gravy with bits. Lumpy surprise with lumps. Gristly glop with globules. Food with its own life slopping about on his tray. NO!

Horrid Henry couldn't face it.
He'd fought so hard for a packed
lunch. Even a packed lunch like the
one Dad made, fortified with eight
essential minerals and vitamins,
was better than going back to
school dinners.

He could, of course, just eat healthy foods. Greta never snatched those. Henry imagined his lunchbox, groaning with alfalfa sprouts on wholemeal brown bread studded with chewy bits.

Ugh. Blecccch! Torture!

He had to keep his packed lunch.
But he had to stop Greta.
He just had to.
And then suddenly Henry had a
brilliant, spectacular idea. It was so
brilliant that for a moment he could
hardly believe he'd thought of it.

Oh boy, Greta, thought Henry gleefully, are you going to be sorry you messed with me.

Chapter 7

Lunchtime.
Horrid Henry sat with his lunchbox
unopened.

Rude Ralph was armed and ready beside him. Now, where was Greta?

Thump. Thump. Thump.
The floor shook as the demon dinner
lady started her food patrol.

Horrid Henry waited until she was
almost behind him. SNAP!
He opened his lunchbox.

SNATCH!

The familiar greasy hand shot
out, grabbed Henry's biscuits and
shovelled them into her mouth.
Her terrible teeth began to chomp.
And then . . .

"Yiaowwww! Aaaarrrgh!"

A terrible scream echoed through the packed lunch room.

Greasy Greta
turned purple.

Then pink.

Then
bright red.

"Yiaowwww!" she howled.
"I need to cool down!
Gimme that!" she screeched,
snatching Rude Ralph's doughnut
and stuffing it in her mouth.

"Aaaarrrgh!" she choked.
"I'm on fire! Water! Water!"
She grabbed a pitcher of water,
poured it on top of herself,
then ran howling down the aisle
and out the door.

For a moment there was silence.
Then the entire packed lunch room
started clapping and cheering.

"Wow, Henry," said Greedy Graham, "what did you do to her?"

"Nothing," said Horrid Henry. "She just tried my special recipe. Hot chilli powder biscuits, anyone?"

What are you going to read next?

More adventures with

or go to
sea with

Horrid Henry,

or into space with

Poppy the Pirate Dog,

You could
have fun
on

Cudweed.

A Rainbow Shopping Day,

or explore

Down in the Jungle,

but watch out for

A Creepy Crawly Story!

Make magic with

The Three Little Witches,

and have
a ball
with

Princesses.

Or follow the star in

The First Christmas.

Enjoy all the Early Readers.

the
orion star

Sign up for **the orion star** newsletter
for all the latest children's book news,
plus activity sheets, exclusive competitions,
author interviews, pre-publication extracts
and more.

www.orionbooks.co.uk/newsletters

Follow @the_orionstar on .